LUTHER'S HALLOWEEN

written by
Cari Meister

illustrated by
Valeria Petrone

VIKING

For Edwin, my Halloween monster—C. M.

For Ximo—V. P.

VIKING

Published by Penguin Group

Penguin Young Readers Group, 345 Hudson Street, New York, New York 10014, U.S.A.

Penguin Books Ltd, 80 Strand, London WC2R 0RL, England

Penguin Books Australia Ltd, 250 Camberwell Road, Camberwell, Victoria 3124, Australia

Penguin Books Canada Ltd, 10 Alcorn Avenue, Toronto, Ontario, Canada M4V 3B2

Penguin Books (N.Z.) Ltd, 182-190 Wairau Road, Auckland 10, New Zealand

First published in 2004 by Viking, a division of Penguin Young Readers Group

10 9 8 7 6 5 4 3 2 1

Text copyright © Cari Meister, 2004

Illustrations copyright © Valeria Petrone, 2004

Library of Congress Cataloging-in-Publication Data is available

ISBN: 0-670-03555-6

Manufactured in China

Set in Clarendon

Book design by Jim Hoover

THIS IS LUTHER.

He is a dinosaur—
a triceratops, to be exact.
You can tell by the little horn on his nose.

Tonight is Halloween.
I'm making Luther's costume.
"Hold still, Luther! I'm almost done."

I'm going to be a scary werewolf.

GRRRR!

At first, Luther is afraid
of my costume. He forgets it's me.

"Luther! Get down from there!
See? It's just me. Let's go!"

There are a lot of trick-or-treaters outside.
Mummies and witches. Frogs and princesses.
Kitty cats and goblins.
There is even a lobster!

At first,
Luther is scared.

But I tell him it's okay.
After all, he's a dinosaur.
Nobody messes with a dinosaur.

Luther is busy licking a
kid dressed up like a ham
when we hear someone scream
"Help!   Help!"

"Look, Luther!" I yell.
"Dracula is stealing
Frankenstein's treat bag!"

"Help!   Help!"

Dracula is stealing the skeleton's treats, too!

Luther and I hide behind a tree.

Well,
sort of.

Just as Dracula walks by,
I count to three
and jump out.

GGRRRRRRR

RRR! I say.

But Dracula doesn't know
about my secret weapon—

Luther!

RROOOAARR!

"Nice try, kid. Aren't you a little old for Halloween?" he says to Luther.

That's when I take off Luther's costume.

Dracula takes one look at Luther
and drops my treat bag.

Dracula tries to run away,
but he is way too slow for Luther.

"Good work, Luther!" I yell.
Everybody is happy.
Everybody except Dracula.

Happy Halloween, Luther!